This is Teacher Tina. She is a great teacher, and she takes her class on lots of interesting trips around Story Town.

Little Workmates

Teacher Tina

by Mandy Ross

illustrated by Emma Dodd

Early one morning,
Teacher Tina set
off for school.

"Mustn't be late!"
she said. "It's the
class trip to
Story Town
Castle today."

TINA 1

"Will we meet Queen Clara?" asked the children.

"I shouldn't think so," said Teacher Tina. "She is a very busy queen."

Teacher Tina set off with her class through Story Town.

"Children, make sure you don't get lost, please," she said.

And no one did.

They crossed the
wooden drawbridge
over the castle moat.

"Children, make sure you
don't fall off, please,"
said Teacher Tina.

And no
one did.

They climbed
up the castle tower.

"Children, make sure you
don't fall off please,"
said Teacher Tina.

And no one did.

They went to see the
castle dungeons.

"Children, make sure you
don't get locked in, please,"
said Teacher Tina.

And no one
did, until...

CLANG

The dungeon door slammed shut. Teacher Tina was locked inside!

"Oh, no!" said Teacher Tina. And then she noticed something gleaming on the floor.

Just then, they heard
footsteps.

"Look!" cried the children.
"It's Queen Clara!"

"Your Majesty," said
Teacher Tina. "I'm afraid
I am locked in your
dungeon—but look I have
found..."

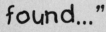

"My crown!" exclaimed Queen Clara. "I lost it again last week. Thank you for finding it!"

And, with a huge key, she opened the dungeon to let Teacher Tina out.

"Please join me for a royal lunch!" said Queen Clara. And she led Teacher Tina and all her class right through the castle to the Royal Dining Room.

"Thank you for finding my crown, Teacher Tina!" said Queen Clara.

"Hurray for Queen Clara!" cried Teacher Tina.

"Hurray" cried all the children, throwing their hats in the air!

"Children, make sure you don't get lost, please," said Teacher Tina, as they set off back to school.

And no one did.

This is Fireman Fergus. He is a brave firefighter and he has a good head for heights.

This is Nurse Nancy. She works hard looking after the patients at Story Town Hospital.

This is Builder Bill. He is a very good builder and his houses never fall down.

This is Queen Clara. She is a very good queen and all the people of Story Town love her.

This is Postman Pete. He loves delivering letters and parcels to everyone in Story Town.